The Wedding Gift

The Wedding Gift

Moshe Goldberger

TARGUM/FELDHEIM

First published 1996
Copyright © 1995 by Moshe Goldberger
ISBN 1-56871-095-X

All rights reserved

No part of this publication may be translated, reproduced, stored in a retrieval system or transmitted, in any form or by any means, electronic, mechanical, photocopying, recording or otherwise, without prior permission in writing from both the copyright holder and the publisher.

Phototypest by: Targum Press
Plates: Frank Jerusalem

Published by:
Targum Press Inc.
22700 W. Eleven Mile Rd.
Southfield, Mich. 48034

Distributed by:
Feldheim Publishers
200 Airport Executive Park
Nanuet, N.Y. 10954

Distributed in Israel by:
Targum Press Ltd.
POB 43170
Jerusalem 91430

Printed in Israel

Contents

Preface 11
Introduction 13

PART ONE: Preparing for Marriage

Rule 1   Count Your Blessings Every Day 17
Rule 2   Love Your Work 19
Rule 3   Ask Questions and Learn 21
Rule 4   Focus on Your Family 22
Rule 5   Believe in Yourself 24
Rule 6   Avoid Pride 26
Rule 7   Prepare for Tests 28
Rule 8   Avoid Clutter 30
Rule 9   Living Each Day 32
Rule 10 Treating Others Respectfully 34
Rule 11 Serve Hashem with Laughter 36
Rule 12 Do Your Best 38
Rule 13 Start Your Day Singing 41
Rule 14 Set Weekly Goals 43
Rule 15 Protect Your Good Mood 45
Rule 16 "This, Too, Is for the Good" 47

| Rule 17 | Formula for Happiness | 50 |
| Rule 18 | To Sum Up | 52 |

PART TWO: The Wedding Gift

Step 1	The Goal	55
Step 2	Questions	58
Step 3	Significant Other	60
Step 4	The Other Half	62
Step 5	More Understanding	64
Step 6	Courtesy	66
Step 7	Thoughtfulness	68
Step 8	Weighing Honor	70
Step 9	The Secret of Prosperity	72
Step 10	Five Minutes	74
Step 11	Paying Attention	76
Step 12	Love of Your Fellowman	78
Step 13	Caring and Sharing	79
Step 14	Sensitivity	80
Step 15	Levels of *Kavod*	82
Step 16	Creative Communication	84
Step 17	Gentleness and Calmness	86
Step 18	The Power of Gentleness	88
Step 19	Heads and Hearts	90
Step 20	Thank You	92

Conclusion 94

Dedication

Dedicated in honor
of my co-author,
best friend, and partner,
my dear wife

Dedication

Dedicated by Moshe Finer

to my wife,
SHIFRA

A constant source of inspiration
to me and our children:
Ashra, Avi, and Hirshi
and to everyone else

Dedication

A dedication from Tuvya

to my dear wife,
TZIPORA

A birthday gift that is a reminder
of our wedding gift
commitment to each other,
on behalf of her constant devotion
to her husband and family.
May she continue to reap
nachas from all of us.

Preface

"Hashem helps those who help themselves," or, in the words of the Talmud, "On the path one is determined to go, he is led [by Hashem]" (*Makos* 10b). We must learn to choose the right direction to take and then advance.

The laws of gravity and physics have been studied and understood to some extent. They work in certain ways and can work for you if you harness them. Similarly, the Torah has principles that we are urged to use for our benefit. These are eternal laws that have always worked, and they are right in front of our eyes for us to recognize and use.

In order to get the most out of this book, we suggest that one begins with the mishnah (*Pirkei Avos* 7) on how to be wise. We will paraphrase some of the teachings of the mishnah for this purpose:

- Admit the truth: "We are not perfect." We may be able to fool others, but Hashem knows we are lacking.
- The sources for this work are from sages who were wiser than us. We should not be embarrassed to accept their teachings. Besides, they are only passing on the teachings of Hashem's Torah. Thus, we should swallow our pride to learn what they teach us.
- "Who is wise? He who learns from all people" (*Pirkei Avos* 4:1). When we realize that we need help from others and listen to them in order to learn, we are already wiser.

We can pray to Hashem for help at any time. Hashem's answer, however, may be: "Why do you think I sent you the very book you have in your hands? Don't you realize I am trying to help you?"

Imagine that you have received a personal note from Hashem with a message that says: "I love you. Don't despair. I am informing you that you need to modify your approach. I have provided you with a map that contains a clear route to guide you. Do your best, and I will continue to help you along. Here are some rules that will remind you of My hopes for you and how to achieve them."

Introduction

Which would you choose: a million dollars in cash, or a penny that will double in value every day for thirty days?

On first impulse, the average person would choose the million dollars. The far wiser choice, however, is the penny that would double itself daily. Although on day six you will have only thirty-two cents, by day twenty-eight you will have accumulated $1,342,177. On day twenty-nine, you will have over $2.6 million.

This demonstrates the compound interest power of positive small steps. The snowball effect, over time, *b'ezras Hashem*, becomes immensely meaningful and fruitful.

The Talmudic rule *"Tofasto mu'at tofasto* — If you grab hold of a small amount, you will achieve" is a fundamental approach to permanent, lasting achievement.

We can paraphrase the Mishnah (*Avos* 2:1) as well: "Be careful with every small mitzvah opportunity, for you do not realize the vast significance of every mitzvah."

Part I:

PREPARING FOR MARRIAGE: HELP YOURSELF!

For personal perfection.
For marriage miracles.
For raising children.

Rule 1

Count Your Blessings Every Day

Rambam ("*Hilchos Tefillah*," chap. 7) teaches the obligation to recite a minimum of one hundred blessings daily. He then explains that if a person falls short on any day, he should be certain to add to his stock of blessings and count all the blessings until he reaches one hundred.

One must learn to appreciate his assets, to count his blessings.

> *Who is wealthy? He who rejoices with his lot.*
> *Pirkei Avos* 4:1

You say a blessing for your eyes every morning: "...Who opens the eyes of the blind." Is that not a most precious asset? Your eyes are surely worth at least a billion dollars.

Next door to where I live there is a family that has a child who is missing most of one arm. Do you have two hands? Would you put a price tag on the value of your limbs? Do you have two legs, two ears, a mind?

Try figuring out the value of your one hundred blessings. That will get you started right any day.

Rule 2

Love Your Work

In conjunction with the first rule of learning to appreciate the countless gifts Hashem showers on you, you must also focus on what it is that you are doing for Him.

What do you produce during your day? Life is too short to complain or waste time.

"Love work" (*Pirkei Avos* 1:10) is a mishnah that most people fail to focus on as an obligation. We know you believe in loving Hashem and your fellowman, but do you realize that Hashem also expects you to love your daily occupation?

Although a person should not think of himself as indispensable — Hashem prefers that you realize you need Him, that He does not need you — Hashem created you because He wants you to achieve a certain goal — to accomplish that which only you can do! If one knows he has a special mission in this world, he finds it easier to love his work. Not only that, but when you do whatever it is you do "for the sake of Heaven," you can achieve daily success, and Hashem will see to it that your compensation includes what you need to pay your bills and then some. *The more you love your work, the more you will get paid.* Try it, and you will enjoy fulfilling the mishnah "Love work."

Rule 3

Ask Questions and Learn

A righteous person falls down seven times, and [still he] rises...

Mishlei 24:16

In order to grow we must learn from our mistakes. A wise person admits his flaws (*Pirkei Avos* 7:9).

The more questions you ask of people who know, the more you will learn. Are you struggling in business? Are you unable to pay your bills? You may not be asking the right people enough questions. When was the last time you made a mistake? Once you admit your mistakes and realize you don't know everything, you will be able to seek advice and work to overcome your flaws. Then you will truly be wise!

Who is wise? He who learns from every person.
Pirkei Avos 4:1

Rule 4
Focus on Your Family

In Shema, we declare that Hashem is our God, Who is in complete control. We then state the obligation to love Him with all we have, to always focus on His Torah, and to teach it diligently to our children.

The best method for teaching our children is to serve as a role model for them. They learn most from our example. They watch everything we do; they listen to everything we say. If we love Hashem, and His Torah and mitzvos, our children will learn from us and do the same.

Why is this so important? Because our life perpetuates itself in our children. If we don't make the effort to be there for our children, how will we teach them what it means to live for Hashem?

Rambam (*Moreh Nevuchim* 3:51) explains that the primary focus in the lives of the Avos was to develop a nation that would serve Hashem. The start of that nation was their very own family.

Avraham Avinu said: "What will You give me? I am childless" (Bereishis 15:2).

And Hashem says to us: "What are you doing for Me? Are you teaching your children diligently to know Me and to love Me?" (see Bereishis 18:14 and Devarim 6:1).

Rule 5

Believe in Yourself

By counting your blessings every day (rule 1), loving your work (rule 2), asking questions (rule 3), and focusing on your family (rule 4), you can achieve great results. But it all begins with your attitude.

When you realize that you are fortunate to have received tons of gifts from Hashem, when you realize that Hashem is surrounding you with opportunities for your benefit, you will be able to achieve great success.

> *Guard your mind more than anything else, for it produces all the results of life.*
>
> Mishlei 4:23

Yes, you are great!

The Gemara (*Sanhedrin* 37a) teaches the obligation for every individual to say, "Hashem created the world because of *me!*"

You have it within yourself to accomplish great deeds. The process begins with the mind Hashem gave you, and it ends with a goal set by Mishlei: "A good mind is at an everlasting feast" (15:15).

Rule 6

Avoid Pride

Caution. Do not deceive yourself. Do not let rule 5 go to your head and lead you to false pride.

The great sage Rabbi Yochanan ben Zakkai, who was the youngest of Hillel's eighty disciples, knew everything. (The Gemara [*Bava Basra* 134a] lists eighteen subjects that he knew, many of which we do not even have an idea of what they are about.) Yet he would always say, "Even if you have studied much Torah, do not take pride in yourself, for that is what you were created for" (*Pirkei Avos* 2:9).

People (yes, me and you) tend to be blinded by a little success, becoming arrogant and thinking they are invincible. This is a temptation that affects all people, and the less you realize how much it affects you, the more it can (or has) influence you.

We also learn from Rabbi Yochanan ben Zakkai

Avoid Pride

how to deal with the problem. He would always review the truth. We have to keep hammering the truth into our minds to keep arrogance from developing.

It is easy to fall into the trap of believing all the nice comments people may say and write and become spoiled by being in the limelight, especially when one is being honored when giving a speech or writing a book. This is why our sages would recite verses that promote humility while they were being honored. For example, when Rav would see people following him, he would repeat verses from Iyov (20:6–7) to himself: "Like his own waste products, he shall be forgotten." (See *Sanhedrin* 7b.)

So, although you must believe in yourself and your potential for success, keep in mind that you are far from perfect.

Rule 7

Prepare for Tests

At times things seem unfair. Why is another person more deserving than you? Of course, you may be in complete error. When you think, "This is a case of 'Why do the righteous sometimes suffer?'" it may in reality be a case of "a wicked person who is receiving great benefits" (Rabbi A. Miller).

Yet there are times when our sages teach us that we are meant to suffer for a good reason. *Mesilas Yesharim* (chap. 1) sums up our purpose in this world in three steps:

- Fulfill mitzvos.
- Serve Hashem.
- To be tested.

Are you going to refuse to give up? Will you resist

defeat and keep trying no matter how difficult your situation? If you keep in mind that Hashem may be testing you, it might be easier to persevere.

A tzaddik falls seven times and rises.
                                            Mishlei 24:16

"Please, Hashem, grant me patience — but I can't wait!"

Rule 8

Avoid Clutter

He did it again.

When you thought you had your evil inclination under control (your proof is all the good you were busy accomplishing), he was actually controlling you! Indeed, his most encompassing method for causing people to lose their perspective in life is to keep them busy — too busy to think clearly (*Mesilas Yesharim*, chap. 5).

> *He puts the world into their hearts so that it is difficult for them to notice Hashem's work.*
> Koheles 3:11

There are groups called "Clutterer's Anonymous" that help people recover from clutter, eliminate the problem, and develop order and purpose in their lives. Some of the questions in their brochure are:

Avoid Clutter

- Do you have more possessions than you can handle?
- Do you find it difficult to dispose of things, even those you never seem to use?
- Do you spend time looking for things you need but cannot find?
- Are you reluctant to put things away in their proper place?
- Are you constantly doing for others while your own home is disorderly?
- Do you get bogged down by menial and unimportant things and thus are unable to focus on the real challenges of life?
- Are you always busy running around with projects, meetings, and errands, which seem to justify why you have to shortchange primary activities, such as Torah study and prayer? Are you "busy" without getting anywhere? Is your life full of clutter but most of it inconsequential? Are you hiding behind petty chores? Are you avoiding to *shteig* because of the new responsibilities that may be involved?

This lesson can be summed up in five words: "Minimize your involvements and study Torah!" (*Pirkei Avos* 4:12).

Rule 9

Living Each Day

> *If not now — when?*
>
> Pirkei Avos 1:14

Now is the time to regret the mistakes of yesterday and prepare for the challenges of tomorrow. This is it. Make today the best day of this month.

Today is the best time to count your blessings (rule 1). Make sure to notice the old ones, as well as the new ones. For example, did you notice that your five fingers are each of a different size and shape?

Today is the day you will love your work and thank Hashem for it (rule 2).

Today you will find a mistake you've made to learn from, or you can review one of your old learning experiences (rule 3).

Today is the day to focus on appreciating one new

Living Each Day

quality of your spouse, to concentrate on the goodness and kindness he/she does for you.

Today you will start that (new) project you have been putting off.

Tell yourself, "Today is a gorgeous day!" (That is what you should be saying every single day.) It is great to be alive!

> *When you grab hold of a small amount, you will succeed.*
>
> Sukkah 5b

You can become a world-class expert on any topic of your choice if you tackle the endeavor one day at a time.

Why did Hashem design days in twenty-four-hour units, weeks in seven-day units, and months that begin with Rosh Chodesh?

One reason is to make it easier for us to live by focusing on each day as a separate entity. Today is precious. Live this day as if it were the only day. Do your best!

Rule 10

Treating Others Respectfully

Just as we must focus on, "Now is the time," so too each person you deal with is a mitzvah relationship for now. Treat everyone you meet as if they are important — because they are!

If you knew that a certain Jew is a descendent of the greatest tzaddik in the world, you would treat him accordingly. Now the secret: he is! Every human being is designed and created in the image of Hashem, and every Jew is considered an offspring of Hashem (Devarim 14:1). This concept is so incredible that we tend to shy away from it. But it is true.

Focus on one Jew at a time, with consideration, care, kindness, and love. Each Jew is extremely important to Hashem. Is that not enough of a recom-

Treating Others Respectfully 35

mendation for us as well?

When you make a person feel important, there is a bonus for you, too: "Who will be honored? He who honors others" (*Pirkei Avos* 4:1). This includes every person, bar none. Make each one feel important, and, measure for measure, Hashem will do the same for you.

When *Pirkei Avos* (2:10) teaches us how to deal with others, three concepts are grouped together:

- Your fellowman's honor should be as beloved to you as your own.
- Do not be quick to anger.
- "Repent the day before you die," which is explained to mean, "Repent *each* day, for it may be the last day of your life!"

We can suggest that these three concepts are dependent on each other. If you would consider today the last day of your life it would affect the way you deal with everyone else. Your dealings with your spouse, parents, neighbors, in-laws, friends, and acquaintances will be different. You certainly wouldn't become angry. You wouldn't hurt a fly. You would be an angel.

Rule 11

Serve Hashem with Laughter

Serve Hashem with joy.

Tehillim 100

Does this mean that only while you are studying Torah, are occupied with some other mitzvah, or doing someone a favor, you should be happy, or does it mean that your service to Hashem should include an independent entity called *simchah*?

A good laugh is a mitzvah. Consider the teaching of *Mesilas Yesharim*, that *simchah* is one of the three components of *ahavah* (love). Thus, the mitzvah to love Hashem is also a mitzvah to be happy. You can refer back to rules 1 and 2 and practice them with this concept in mind.

But isn't life serious business? Yes, it is, and that's

Serve Hashem with Laughter

why this is no laughing matter. Those who make people happy are destined to great rewards in *olam habba* (Taanis 21b). And it starts with being happy yourself.

To laugh, one must learn to ignore the pettiness of insults and errors and not to take trivial things too seriously.

As a matter of fact, we can prove that Hashem desires that we practice being happy from an explicit verse in the first chapter of the Torah (Bereishis 1:31): "When God saw all that He had created..." (Now how would we expect Hashem to react at the first historical "performance review" of His creation of the universe? Would we expect Hashem to clap in some form?)

Hashem is teaching us for all time, "...And behold it was all very good." This lesson should make us all rejoice heartily.

Laugh a little and enjoy the good fortune
Hashem is bombarding you with!

Rule 12

Do Your Best

According to the difficulty [of the task], so is the reward.

Pirkei Avos 5:23

When we serve Hashem with meticulous concern for perfection, we merit tremendous rewards. Therefore, there is no such thing as a small mitzvah.

Be as careful with easy mitzvos as with difficult ones.

Pirkei Avos 2:1

One should recognize the importance of every mitzvah, big and small.

Do small things matter? They most certainly do. Because you are so special, Hashem created you with the power, responsibility, and privilege that every act you do influences the entire universe. If this concept is new to you, you might want to study the first section of the *sefer Nefesh HaChayim* (or our booklet on the subject, *The Enormous Power You Possess*).

Every minute difference has eternal consequences. Every small act is actually big. In addition, one mitzvah leads to the next. When you do your best, Hashem helps you do even better. The extra effort you put in will be worth your while in ways you cannot imagine.

> *One time with difficulty is worth more than 100 times without difficulty.*
> *Avos D'Rabbi Nassan* 3:6

If you encourage yourself to be disciplined and push for one more review when you are about to give up in frustration, you will achieve extraordinary gain. Who will know the difference? Hashem will, and that's what counts the most.

> *There is no comparison between one who studies 100 times and one who studies 101 times.*
> *Chagigah 9b*

How can you do your best?
- Focus (see rule 8).
- Work on one small thing at a time (see rule 9).
- Be determined (see "Preface").

*   *   *

> *And in all that he did, Hashem caused him to succeed.*
>
> Bereishis 39:3

Yosef understood that Hashem devises and controls every circumstance, and thus he made the best of his life at every step. Everything he did was with diligence and energy, in accordance with Hashem's ways (*The Beginning* 569).

Rule 13

Start Your Day Singing

Every day is another opportunity to improve on yesterday. What is the best way to start your day? With songs to Hashem. The *"Pesukei D'Zimra"* section of our daily morning prayers consists of verses of song that can help you get started on the road to a great day. The way you start your day can make all the difference in getting you motivated to be positive, powerful, productive, and tuned into Hashem.

There is one starter phrase we say every morning that can do the trick even by itself. This technique may be so much a part of your routine that you may not realize how to utilize it properly. It can turn on the sunshine and music even on a cloudy day and even if the birds are not singing.

All you have to do is say *"Modeh Ani"* with an understanding of the words: "I am grateful to You

Hashem...for returning my *neshamah* (breath of life and my soul) to me...." Consider how many people did not wake up this morning. They would have been absolutely delighted to be in your shoes, even with all your aggravations, doubts, and problems. Life is the most precious gift there is, and yet the wealthiest person in the world cannot buy more time the day his life is not returned to him by the Creator.

Thank Hashem that you are here today!

Rule 14

Set Weekly Goals

One of the fundamental lessons we learn from Hashem's declaration that this world is "very good" (see rule 11) is to emulate the Creator by taking stock of our progress every week. The world is full of joy, and we are required to step back and appreciate it in order to give thanks to Hashem.

Setting big goals is too easy, because it does not require much thought and we feel proud of our accomplishment. The harder and more successful approach is to set small, satisfying goals. Setting reachable goals — even daily and weekly ones — will motivate us to keep going.

Mesilas Yesharim defines life as the opportunity to fulfill mitzvos, serve Hashem, and withstand ordeals (see rule 7). Thus, every day is a grand gift of opportunities galore from the Creator of the Universe. To succeed, we must focus daily on goals that will enable us to reach our potential for that day.

Who is wealthy? He who rejoices with his lot.
Pirkei Avos 4:1

This means to rejoice daily with the special gifts that Hashem has provided you with — today!

Are you able to walk unaided to the door of your house? Is that not wealth? Is not your arm a treasured possession? Do you own a tallis and tefillin? The tefillin are worth more than a golden crown studded with precious gems. The tallis, too, is a garment that proclaims its wearer a servant of the Almighty. Thus, you are one of the most successful people that exist in this world. You are a member of the greatest people that ever walked on the earth.

True happiness (in this world) is to enjoy that which one possesses in the present, with the satisfaction of knowing that the One and Only, Who loves you, has provided you with a portion that is perfectly suited to your immediate needs.

Set short-term goals for each day of the week, with the long-term plan to be able to sit back on Shabbos and sing praise to Hashem for helping you serve Him this week in the very best manner that He expects from you.

Rule 15

Protect Your Good Mood

People cannot ruin your mood unless you permit them to. Your time is too precious to waste on sadness, gloom, despair, envy, jealousy, or hatred.

A slight mishap can be troubling and disturbing if we allow it to be. Harsh words from others, a traffic jam, or a stain can ruin one's whole day, but "a good mind is at an everlasting feast" (Mishlei 15:15). You can learn to ignore distractions and remain happy. You can be determined to rejoice and keep doing your best no matter what.

> *Do not hold a grudge against your people.*
> VaYikra 19:18

> *This enables people to keep on dealing with one another.*
> Rambam, "Hilchos Deos" 7:8

We must also learn to avoid those people who, like fools, may test our mind-set (Mishlei 17:12), and deal with every situation in a positive way.

Appreciate the time Hashem has given you. How precious is a minute of your time?

> *What is a minute?*
> *Sixty seconds are in it.*
> *You cannot refuse it.*
> *It's up to you to use it.*
> *There are consequences if you lose it*
> *Or abuse it.*
> *Every tiny little minute*
> *Has eternity in it.*
> *It is actually infinite!*

Rule 16

"This, Too, Is for the Good"

How many of your daily sayings are a fulfillment of a law in the *Shulchan Aruch*? Here is one that is relatively simple to learn, and it can be used daily with ease and benefits galore. "One should always say, 'All that the Merciful One does is for the good.'" (See *Shulchan Aruch* 230:5.)

Wow! That is a mouthful when you think about it. Do you believe that nothing bad has ever happened to you? (If you say yes, I won't believe you.)

I am not accusing you of not fulfilling a law of the *Shulchan Aruch*. It does not say you have to believe it. That takes years and years of work. The mitzvah is to *say* it repeatedly until it becomes a reflex.

The word *"le'olam"* ("one should always...") has three meanings:

- This is the most ideal statement.
- It has to be repeated constantly and eternally.
- The root of the word implies concealment. Say it even when it does not seem so.

Ma'amar Mordechai 27

To test this premise, we can ask regarding this lesson itself: "Why did Hashem send me this powerful message now? Why not earlier on in my career? Why didn't such a 'good' thing happen earlier on to such a good person (namely, 'me')?"

It may not have been good for you to learn this lesson earlier. One who discovers a treasure when he is not ready to appreciate it suffers in that its value is never fully appreciated and causes its owner harm.

Adversity has a way of teaching lessons that would never have been discovered without it. Thus, not knowing beneficial information can also serve as a benefit at times. But Hashem is allowing you to read this now. That's terrific. No more excuses.

If we train ourselves to say the above message again and again, Hashem will assist us to understand why a particular incident is for the good. It may take

"This, Too, Is for the Good" 49

awhile, and a bit of thought, to actually discover the good, but know that it is there.

When one door shuts, another door has already been opened by Hashem: "The cure is prepared before the ailment" (*Megillah* 13b). Search for the good in adversity, but begin the process by declaring that it exists.

"Everything Hashem does for us is good." That is how to react to problems. That is how to turn defeat into victory — by discovering the benefits Hashem has intended. The test of life is to say this formula even when it is the most difficult thing to say.

Rule 17
Formula for Happiness

The Torah and its commentators are loaded with formulas for happiness.

> *Who is wealthy? He who rejoices with his lot.*
> Pirkei Avos 4:1

What should we focus on in life? What should we be working on day in and day out?

Are we seeking happiness? Are we searching for elusive intangibles such as peace and contentment in ways that are unproven?

Can making money be the key to happiness? Not if the person fails to learn how to rejoice with his lot. Acquiring real estate or collecting valuable objects has the same problem.

To enjoy life, one must learn to train himself to rejoice with what he possesses at any given moment.

Formula for Happiness

You cannot buy happiness with money. Where can one buy it? One can acquire happiness by training oneself to think correct thoughts.

When? The time to be happy is now!
Where? The place where you are now!
How? You already know how.

Rabbi Tuvia Goldstein, *shlita*, quoted, at a *shiur*, the following message he once saw engraved on a tombstone:

> *You are where I was*
> *I am where you will be*
> *Torah and mitzvos I took with me*
> *The rest I left for you*

Rule 18

To Sum Up

The first and most basic of the cardinal "*Ani Ma'amins*" is to believe with complete, steadfast *emunah* that the Creator, may His Name be blessed, is the One and Only Creator and Controller of all, and it is He alone Who has done all, is doing all now, and continues to do all forever. To this, we add the teaching that everything He does is for the good!

Looks, however, are deceiving. To feel and understand this principle and to relate it to our daily lives takes a lifetime of learning, part of which comes in the form of hard knocks. And that, too, is for the good.

Part II:
THE WEDDING GIFT

A twenty-step program to help you achieve
the "wealth of marriage"
by honoring your spouse.

Step 1

The Goal

Is there a secret to improving one's marriage? What is the key that will help both husband and wife work things out together with less friction?

Rambam (*"Hilchos Ishus,"* 15:19–20) lists seven principles each spouse should follow for a good marriage:

The husband is instructed to:	**The wife is instructed to:**
Treat her with more honor than he would treat himself.	Honor him greatly.
Love her as much as he loves himself.	Hold him in esteem.

Increase benefits to her according to his finances.	Follow his instructions.
Avoid imposing fear upon her.	Think of him as a dignitary.
Speak to her in a kind, gentle manner.	Think of him as a king.
Avoid moodiness.	Conduct herself according to his heart's desire.
Avoid anger.	Avoid doing that which he dislikes.

Although the guidelines for husband and wife are not identical, Rambam begins both sides with the same word: *kavod* (respect).

Learn to treat your spouse as a special person, as if there was a sign on him/her: "Handle with care and respect."

In order to develop this ability (which in itself is a great level), Hashem instructs us: "It is not good for man to be alone; I will make a helpmate for him" (Bereishis 2:18). And then "he should cling to his wife" (*ibid*. 2:24).

Thus, it is the Creator of the Universe Himself

Who has placed His sign of approval, so to speak, on the marriage relationship. Through marriage, one learns to honor and respect another person.

Step 2

Questions

Do you feel that the message of "Step 1: The Goal" does not apply to you personally?

Is it too simple? Too obvious?

Ask yourself why.

Is it because you have already spent years working to perfect your ability to respect your spouse? "Our love for each other is so strong," you may say. "Why do I need to study and work on this subject?"

According to *Pirkei Avos* (chap. 5), there are two types of love: (1) that which will endure, and (2) that which will not endure.

It is essential for everyone to learn how to develop the love that will endure, for that is the fulfillment of the mitzvah of marriage.

What does it mean to really care about someone else? How does one demonstrate honor and respect

Questions

for another person? How does one fulfill, "Forsake his father and mother and cling to his wife" (Bereishis 2:24)?

You do not have to read further if you already know the answers to the following questions:

- How can you make someone feel that they are precious and valuable to you?
- How can you communicate successfully with someone who may interpret things different than you?
- How can you train yourself to praise and compliment another person with sincerity?
- How can you develop the ability to see things from another person's point of view?

If you don't have "the right answers" — and very few of us do — continue to step 3.

Step 3

Significant Other

Who is the most important person in your life? (Before you finalize your answer to this question, spend some time focusing on the verse in Bereishis 2:24: "...and cling to his wife.")

Is your job/work/hobby more important to you than your spouse?

Our sages compare a wife to Torah study. There are many whose eyes light up and their personalities brim with excitement when they are involved in studying Torah. But have they developed a similar feeling of genuine excitement in their ongoing relationship with their spouses? Granted, the mitzvah to love Hashem's Torah is included in the fundamental mitzvah, "To love Hashem, your God, with all your heart" (Devarim 6:5). But one can counter with the realization that the mitzvah to love your spouse is also included in a fundamental mitzvah that is considered the summary of the *entire* Torah: "Love your fellow Jew as yourself" (VaYikra 19:18).

*   *   *

Who can find an excellent wife, whose value is worth far more than jewels?

Mishlei 31:10

We sing this verse on Friday nights and think that it comes easily to us. We get married, and voila, we have merited the true *eishes chayil*. But to fully benefit from the potential *eishes chayil* you have married, you must do some soul-searching into your ways of appreciating and treating her.

Step 4

The Other Half

Why is marriage such a great challenge? "I've done a good job taking care of myself in the past, why can't I do the same for both of us now?"

We all know the Talmudic dictum: "His wife is like himself" (*Berachos* 24a). So why should there be friction, resentment, or misunderstanding?

But that is part of the problem!

Because a man considers his wife part of himself, he wants to treat her as if she were a man.

Most people do not really know the other side of themselves:

> *Women are a nation by themselves.*
>
> Shabbos 62a

It is as if women are created from a different substance, as if they are made from bone (man's bone)

The Other Half

and men, from earth (*Niddah* 31b). In other words, it is as if they each come from different planets.

Thus, the ability to honor and respect one's wife (even in ordinary situations) is a challenge that many people fail to achieve. This explains Rava's teaching: "Honor your wife so that you will become wealthy" (*Bava Metzia* 59a). Not everyone is wealthy because it is not that easy. Similarly, to see your wife's point of view takes considerable work and training. It also generates financial wealth and the wealth of understanding other people.

Step 5

More Understanding

Women have extra understanding.
                                Niddah 31

The unique differences between men and women, when they are recognized and appreciated, can serve as steppingstones to a helpful and meaningful relationship. However, when these differences are not understood, they may result in:

- Frequent, sarcastic criticism toward one another.
- Lack of attention toward one another.
- Difficulty in deciding who does what.
- Questions as to what is primary and what is secondary.

More Understanding

It becomes very difficult, if not impossible, for a man to fulfill his obligation "to honor [his wife] more than himself" (*Yevamos* 62b).

When the Gemara says women are from different *nations* (*Shabbos* 62a), it does not say that they are merely from different *families*, rather that they are *totally* different.

Scientists can demonstrate that men and women differ in every cell of their bodies. Their chromosomes are combined in different ways. Their metabolism, skeletal structures, internal organs, hormones, skin, hair, and blood all have basic differences. When Hashem provides each spouse with the grand gift of the other, it is unique in every sense.

Once one realizes how unique his spouse is he will learn to focus on the other's point of view without letting his own perceptions get in the way.

Step 6

Courtesy

It has been said that the fundamental secret to a happy marriage is to practice the three C's — courtesy, courtesy, and courtesy (in other words, communication, consideration, and compromise.)

The Mishnah teaches the secret to all relationships:

> *Who is honorable? He who honors others.*
> Pirkei Avos 4:1

Which person has to begin to demonstrate honor to the other party? The answer is both of them. Every person is required to be courteous to others, never taking anyone for granted.

The obligation to be courteous and respectful to a spouse is even more obligatory than to a stranger. The immense debt of gratitude each has to the other increases the obligation a thousandfold. Therefore, mutual respect, thoughtfulness, and sensitivity is an objective each spouse must work on increasing day after day. The more effort you put in, the more you will receive in return.

When people treat you with courtesy and respect, you like them and enjoy being around them. When you think about it, gentleness and courtesy to one's spouse should also be common sense, and it works to enhance a marriage, making it a warm and beautiful relationship.

Step 7

Thoughtfulness

In the Rambam's list (see "Step 1: The Goal"), we find four positive obligations of a husband toward his wife:

1. Honor.
2. Love.
3. Spending money on her behalf.
4. Speaking gently.

We can suggest that spending money and speaking gently are manifestations of the first two obligations.

Consider a husband who would rather be at work, with other friends, or involved in other activities than spend time with his wife. If something comes up to interfere with your current plans, what endeavors do you push aside more readily? Do activities with or for your wife tend to fall by the wayside?

When making plans, you surely say, "If Hashem wills it," but do you ever add, "and if my wife is willing, too"?

When you do spend time together, is it with consideration and enthusiasm, or is it just routine?

The Mishnah (*Pirkei Avos* 1:15) teaches us to greet every person with a thoughtful, pleasant countenance. Is there any reason not to fulfill this three-part admonition — (1) *sever*, to show feeling and thought, (2) *panim*, show your face and interest, (3) *yafos*, pleasantness — at least once a day, to our spouses? One way to practice this is by considering your spouse as a special visitor or client whom you desire to impress.

Step 8

Weighing Honor

Rambam says, "He should honor her more than himself...and she should honor him excessively..." What does this mean? How does one gauge honor?

Honor means to attach high value, worth, and importance to someone. "*Kavod*" (honor) and "*kaveid*" (heavy) are of the same Hebrew root. How "heavy" is the value of that person to you? That which is more important deserves more honor.

When the Torah says: "Therefore, a man should forsake his father and mother and cling to his wife" (Bereishis 2:24), we wonder, "What about the mitzvah of 'honoring your father and mother' (Shemos 20:27)? Isn't that also one of the greatest of the Torah's commandments?"

Why does the Torah seem to be abrogating one's relationship toward one's parents in order to emphasize the obligation to a spouse? What, theoretically, should one do if both his parents and his spouse need him at the same time?

The answer can be derived from a mishnah (*Bava Metzia* 33a), which teaches that retrieving one's own lost item takes precedence over retrieving one's father's lost item. We see that a person is considered his own closest relative, and thus he is obligated to take care of his own needs first. The gemara in *Keddushin* 2b says, "It is the way of a man to go searching for a wife, for she is a portion of himself that he has lost." Thus, we understand that "forsaking" one's parents is not a lack of respect to them; rather it is the mitzvah to find and develop one's complete self that takes precedence. It is the greatest desire of our parents that we should achieve and develop ourselves. It is their pleasure when we "forsake" them by marrying and developing our own family.

Step 9

The Secret of Prosperity

> *Honor your wife so that you will become wealthy.*
>
> Bava Metzia 59a

What connection is there between making money and honoring one's wife?

People who are financially successful will tell you their secret. They do not tell their customers, "I need to make a profit today. Please buy from me." Rather, the more they help people get what they want and need, the more money people will pay them for their services.

When you redirect your focus from trying to get what you want, to helping other people get what *they* want, you will succeed financially.

This is also the secret of a happy marriage. To

The Secret of Prosperity

honor your wife, you must learn to pay attention to *her* needs and honor her in ways she will appreciate, including treating her with recognition, admiration, and courtesy. These efforts will be rewarded by Hashem in many ways, including financial success.

Looking back to the Rambam's list of the many levels of courtesy in marriage, we readily understand that customers will also like dealing with you when you honor, respect, and love them as the Torah requires of you. When you also demonstrate your feelings by providing them with better quality and service, they will appreciate you even more.

People are sensitive to how you provide them with your services. If you seem angry all the time, deal in a gruff manner, or shout and bark, they shy away from you and do business elsewhere. Similarly, if you speak to your wife gently and in a kind manner, you will reap great reward.

Caring for your spouse and caring for your customers are similar skills — and they both provide abundant results.

Step 10

Five Minutes

When was the last time you spent five minutes thinking about the good qualities of your spouse?

In five minutes you can uncover many precious qualities if you focus on finding them. *Chovos HaLevovos* (section 6:6) tells the story of a wise individual who chanced upon an animal carcass. As others were complaining about the awful stench, he admired its white teeth. He focused on the positive, while others saw only the negative.

Arrogance tends to blind people to the virtues of others. But when we strive to be humble and dwell on others' virtues, they become evident.

One way to focus on the good is to consider that you and your spouse are unique. Hashem has created each of you to unique specifications up to (or down to) your smallest fingerprint. Consider that Hashem has created the entire universe for the person sharing your home with you. Be thankful to Hashem and focus on appreciating at least some of the benefits He has provided you with.

Step 11

Paying Attention

One of the greatest forms of honor and respect is to pay attention to our spouses. At times we may listen to them carefully yet fail to hear the message they are trying to tell us. Their actual words may be concealing the true meaning and intention. For example:

"You *always* do that."

"You *never* do such and such."

When you analyze the intent of the statement, you realize it is not literally "always" or "never." Look past the surface to understand the real message.

> *Fortunate is one who listens and ignores; a hundred evils will pass him by.*
>
> Sanhedrin 7a

One has to become a selective listener, to know

which words to ignore: "She does not mean it literally; she is hurting." Asking her about her day and *really* listening to the answer is a kindness that can make it all worth her while — and yours.

Step 12

Love of Your Fellowman

In order to understand one's obligation toward a spouse, it is incumbent to begin with the study of the mitzvah to love another Jew (VaYikra 19:18).

Rambam ("*Hilchos Deos*" 6:3) defines the mitzvah: "Every person has a mitzvah to love every Jew as oneself...and thus one is required: (a) to praise others, (b) to care for their possessions as one cares for his own possessions, and (c) to care for their honor as one desires *kavod*..."

Thus, each spouse is obligated to compliment and praise the other spouse regularly (i.e., daily or weekly), care for the other's concerns, and honor and respect the other's ways of doing things.

Step 13

Caring and Sharing

We learn that caring for the possessions of others is included in the mitzvah of loving and honoring them. Thus we have uncovered another insight in understanding this secret of prosperity, that honoring your wife leads to becoming wealthy (see step 9).

Since honoring one's wife includes caring for her possessions and supplying her with benefits according to his financial capacity, he will be rewarded, measure for measure, with an increase of wealth.

Step 14

Sensitivity

As an example of caring, let us consider Rambam's last principle in his list of a husband's marriage obligations: avoid anger.

Does this principle belong in Rambam's laws of marriage? It has already been discussed in *"Hilchos Deos"* as part of the teachings on how to be a mensch (decent person).

> *A gentle response turns away anger, but a harsh word stirs up wrath.*
>
> Mishlei 15:1

There is a special obligation for a husband not to get angry. The manner in which one speaks and the emotions one displays triggers reactions in those who are present; anger provokes others to react negatively.

An angry person tends to assert his feelings and

Sensitivity

desires. But the objective of marriage is not to find a way to have more of one's physical needs met. This false notion leads to growing conflict between two selves, each of whom wants his own needs met before considering the needs of the other.

Whose needs are primary and whose are secondary?

One must consider the feelings and desires of his spouse. Thus, the prohibition to anger is of special potency in this regard. Marriage dictates "oneness," which excludes anger. This also explains the caution against moodiness and depression.

In "*Hilchos Deos*" (2:7), where Rambam teaches the principle of refraining from sadness in general, he underscores: "The sages have instructed: one should not be overly frivolous or sad and depressed; rather, one should receive all others with a thoughtful, pleasant countenance."

One has to develop the attitude that his spouse is most important and be eager to share his time and resources with her, to be "נושא בעול," willing to help carry her load in life.

When we empathize with each other by understanding and identifying with others' feelings — by putting ourselves into their situation from their viewpoint with genuine concern — we will be cured of depression.

Step 15

Levels of Kavod

At this point, I will risk asking a question that may provoke heated discussions. I do not mean to point a finger or hurt anyone's feelings, so imagine an abstract situation.

The mishnah teaches three levels of honor:

> *The honor of your disciple should be as dear to you as your own.*
>
> *The honor of your colleague should be like the fear of your rebbe.*
>
> *The fear of your rebbe should be like the fear of Heaven.*
>
> Pirkei Avos 4:16

How does the Torah categorize the ideal respectful relationship between a husband and a wife? As one colleague acts toward another colleague? As a rebbe treats a *talmid* or vice versa?

From Rambam's list of matrimonial obligations, it seems that the man's obligation to respect his wife is greater than the obligation of a rebbe toward a disciple but maybe less than that of a colleague. Her obligation to him is open-ended — maybe the second level of the mishnah.

This may vary depending on the particular situation, but one can also suggest that Hashem has designed marriage relationships, with each party having certain strengths and abilities. Thus, in certain ways, each spouse is a disciple of the other, and in other ways, a rebbe of the other. Their *kavod* obligations may fluctuate based on various elements.

A spouse can be the most available person to learn from. Thus, the spouse becomes a teacher in many ways.

> *Who is wise? He who learns from every person.*
>
> Pirkei Avos 4:1

My wife may be my rebbe in patience, kindliness, and child-rearing, and I can be her rebbe in halachah, *bitachon*, and seeing the "big picture."

Step 16

Creative Communication

Learning from others requires motivation. To teach another person, it helps if one learns how to motivate that person to desire to learn.

Imagine that you came across this work and read through it with interest. You feel that your spouse would also benefit from reading this work. But you are concerned. If you say to him/her, "You need this," you may cause resentment, disinterest, or even a quarrel. Do not say: "Do you have time now to discuss an important matter?" (That sounds like: "I need a favor from you.") However, if you can figure out a way to arouse your spouse's curiosity...

When we reflect on how Rava taught people to honor their wives, we notice something amazing. He did not say: "You must honor your wives; it is a Torah obligation of the highest order." Instead he said: "...so that you will become wealthy" (*Bava Metzia* 59a). (Imagine how excited his congregants and disciples were to get home to further their career by honoring their spouses!)

Try using Rava's technique on your spouse.

Suggestions:
- "Did you see this amazing work?"
- "Do you know what this work says about how to achieve wealth?"
- "Do you think this could work for us?"
- "This remarkable work cost less than ten dollars, but I feel as if it is worth ten million!"
- "Wow! This book has helped me understand what makes our relationship tick. I wish I would have received this book (or a similar work) as a gift ten years ago when we were first married!"

By asking questions that generate interest, one can help others fulfill the mishnah: "Drink their words with thirst" (*Pirkei Avos* 1:4).

Step 17
Gentleness and Calmness

Rambam lists the principles of speaking gently and avoiding anger separately.

What is the difference between the two?

> *Do not rush to anger.*
>
> Koheles 7:9

> *The words of a wise person, when spoken with gentleness, will be accepted.*
>
> Koheles 9:17

These two principles are illustrations of "turn away from evil and do good" (Tehillim 34:15).

Anger is generally evil. Gentleness and calmness is the positive approach to having one's words accepted.

When the Rambam comments on the art of teach-

Gentleness and Calmness 87

ing Torah in *"Hilchos Deos"* (2:5), he states: "Do not respond quickly, and do not speak much; teach in a gentle manner without shouting or elaboration, as Shlomo says: 'The words of the wise, when spoken with gentleness, are accepted.' "

Thus, calmness is not merely a requirement of courtesy, but it is also essential for communicating the message. With it, the message will be received; but not without it!

Step 18

The Power of Gentleness

Why is gentle speech so powerful?
Why do people listen with eagerness when you speak in a gentle manner?

Why does a soft tongue wield the power to even "break bones" and melt hearts? (See Mishlei 25:15.)

Imagine for a moment if a man would practice, even for one day, Rambam's formula for a husband to (a) honor his wife more than himself, (b) love her as himself, (c) use his money for her benefit, and (d) not to impose excessive fear upon her. Subsequently, he would ask her for a favor in a gentle way. How would she respond?

The answer is obvious. She'll be more than eager to please him in every way. He deserves it. Kindness begets kindness. As a matter of fact, she will find herself fulfilling the corresponding principles the

Rambam prescribes for women without even studying the Rambam.

Your gentleness is a strong statement that demonstrates your concern for someone else's feelings. The more you value something, the more gently you deal with that item. If you were handling a $10,000 vase, you would be very gentle because of its great value. Every person you deal with deserves at least the same concern and gentleness — especially your spouse.

Step 19

Heads and Hearts

Let's look back to see how our feelings correspond to the logic of this study.

Rambam puts the obligation to honor one's spouse before that of love and fear, because feelings are more difficult to control.

To perform small, kind acts for another person is within everyone's reach, even those who feel somewhat resentful towards the other person. It will still help build a more fulfilling and loving relationship.

Here are some guidelines for focusing on which small acts of kindness are most beneficial:

Ask yourself:
- How can I cause my spouse to feel more respected and important?
- How can I better understand my spouse's feelings and needs?

Heads and Hearts

- How can I express and feel sincere appreciation towards my spouse on a consistent basis?

As with all Torah teachings, we should not expect to change overnight, and surely not expect others to change in ten minutes. "The benefits...are gained from repetition with constant persistence" (*Mesilas Yesharim*, "Preface"). The more we focus on these truths and study them with inspiration, the more we will understand and feel them, and practice them with more sincerity.

Step 20

Thank You

How does one love another person?

Number one on Rambam's list of loving a person (*"Hilchos Deos"* 6:3) is to compliment and praise him. How does one do this?

The process includes saying the words "thank you" in a caring, thoughtful way.

But what is there to be grateful for? is a thought that may cross our minds at times. This brings us back to the "white teeth" lesson. (See "Step 10: Five Minutes.") If we search for the good, we will find it. Even a carcass can have a redeeming factor, like shiny, white teeth. For example, one who is slow may be cautious, attentive to detail, more creative, and careful to do things perfectly. One who is quick may be easygoing, alert, and energetic.

When was the last time you thanked your spouse

for agreeing to marry you? (That is one favor for which you owe appreciation to each other and to Hashem for the rest of your life.) Then there are countless benefits you receive from one another, including food, clothing, shelter, children, encouragement, and companionship.

However, we must beware the trap of trusting in people instead of Hashem.

> *To Hashem alone my soul hopes; from Him comes my salvation. He alone is my stronghold and my salvation, my fortress... Trust in Him at all times... Pour out your hearts before Him. Kindness is from You; You compensate each person according to his deeds.*
> (Tehillim)

The more we learn to trust in Hashem for everything, the more we will be able to honor and appreciate the spouse He provided us. Slowly but surely, we can elevate ourselves and transform our marriages into a fulfillment of "rejoice with your spouse" (Mishlei 5:18).

Conclusion

The Talmud teaches that one should take leave of his fellowman with a halachic lesson, for that will cause a positive and long-term remembrance.

Why are we reluctant to take leave of others? Because we have enjoyed spending time with them and have benefitted from their company.

Our relationship can be extended. This book can be kept at your side. You can review a lesson a day and jot down your own comments on the margins to make it more personal. You can also drop us a note and share your thoughts with us directly. (If you prefer to send us your copy with your comments marked in, we will return it to you or send you a new copy).

The results you achieve from now on are up to

Conclusion

you. We have tried to be of help, but you have to take this book and carry it over the finish line into your heart and mind. It will take determination, time, and effort; but Hashem will help you.

> *In the way one is determined to go, Hashem will lead him.*
>
> Makos 10b

הוי דן כל אדם לכף זכות

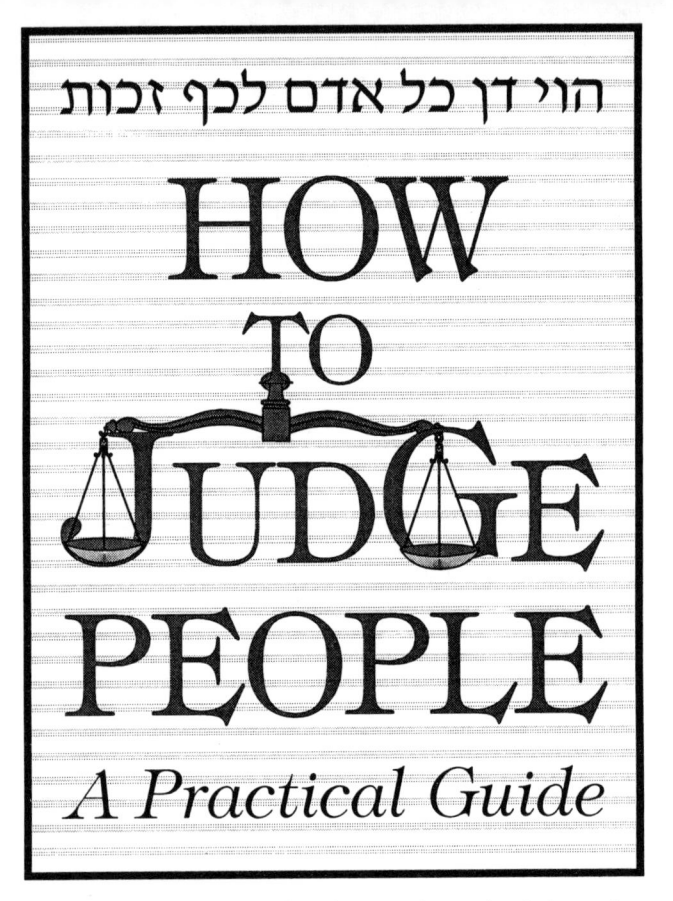

HOW TO JUDGE PEOPLE

A Practical Guide

This concise, readable book examines the injunction to judge our fellow Jews favorably, showing how to apply it to our everyday lives. Anyone concerned with proper behavior towards others will find this an invaluable addition to his library.

A TARGUM PRESS Book
Distributed by **FELDHEIM Publishers**
200 Airport Executive Park, Nanuet, N.Y. 10954 Tel. 1-800-237-7149